The Wishing Horse

"It's a lot of money so this had better work!" snarled the king, as he handed over five hundred gold pieces from the chest which stood near his throne. "Now I wish for lots of gold!"

The old man nodded, went over to Albert and whispered in his ear.

And Albert said, "Neigh."

There was a sudden flash of lightning in the room and . . .

Four more Young Hippo Magic stories to enjoy:

My Friend's a Gris-Quok!
Malorie Blackman

The Little Pet Dragon
Philippa Gregory

Broomstick Services
Ann Jungman

The Marmalade Pony
Linda Newbery

Dare you try a Young Hippo Spooky?

The Screaming Demon Ghostie
Jean Chapman

Scarem's House
Malcolm Yorke

Laugh with a Young Hippo Funny!

Bod's Mum's Knickers
Peter Beere

Emily H and the Enormous Tarantula
Emily H and the Stranger in the Castle
Kara May

MALCOLM YORKE

The Wishing Horse

Illustrated by Jan Lewis

Scholastic Children's Books,
Scholastic Publications Ltd,
7–9 Pratt Street, London NW1 0AE, UK

Scholastic Inc.,
555 Broadway, New York, NY 10012-3999, USA

Scholastic Canada Ltd,
123 Newkirk Road, Richmond Hill,
Ontario, Canada L4C 3G5

Ashton Scholastic Pty Ltd,
P O Box 579, Gosford, New South Wales,
Australia

Ashton Scholastic Ltd,
Private Bag 94407, Greenmount, Auckland,
New Zealand

First published in the UK by Scholastic Publications Ltd, 1995

Text copyright © Malcolm Yorke, 1995
Illustrations copyright © Jan Lewis, 1995

ISBN 0 590 13254 7

Typeset by Contour Typesetters, Southall, London
Printed by Cox & Wyman Ltd, Reading, Berks

10 9 8 7 6

Chapter 1

Long ago and far away in another country, there was an old man and a horse. The horse pulled a battered cart which had a notice painted on the side saying:

ALBERT THE MAGIC HORSE
WISHES GRANTED
500 GOLD PIECES
EACH
EVERY ONE A WINNER

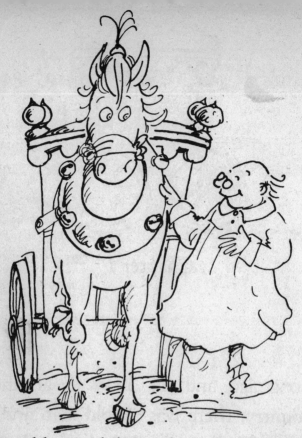

The old man didn't ride in the cart but walked alongside the horse and talked to him.

"I don't think many folk in this miserable place will be able to pay five hundred gold pieces, do you, Albert?"

And Albert said, "Neigh!"

Indeed, the country they were travelling through looked very poor. The roads were full of holes, the cottages were all falling down, the crops were neglected and the cattle looked thin and hungry.

As the old man and Albert were walking along, they met a young man coming towards them. He was dressed in rags and his shoes had many holes in them.

The old man asked him, "Is it far to your main city, young man?"

"About two hours' journey down this road," he replied, "but I wouldn't go there if you can avoid it."

"Why not?" asked the old man.

"Because our selfish king lives there and he's the greediest man on earth. He's just mad about gold. If he sees your old horse and cart he'll make you pay

taxes on them. He taxes everything just so he can live in luxury, counting his gold pieces."

"Oh, dear, he doesn't sound a very nice character," said the old man.

And Albert said, "Neigh."

But they both continued down the road to the big city.

ALBERT THE MAGIC HORSE
WISHES GRANTED
500 GOLD PIECES EACH
EVERY ONE A WINNER.

Soon they overtook a bent old woman hobbling along with a stick, and again the old man asked the way.

"Oh, don't go to the city," she said, "you'll get robbed of everything you've got like I did, and all my family."

"Whoever would rob a poor old man like me?" he asked.

"Well, if the king doesn't rob you the queen will. She's so vain and greedy she's robbed us all just to pay for her fancy necklaces and rings and brooches and jewels."

"She doesn't sound very pleasant, does she?" the old man said, as they plodded on.

And Albert said, "Neigh."

A little further on a boy and girl were sitting by the roadside. They were very skinny, poorly dressed and barefoot. When the old man asked them how near the big city was they told him it was just over the next hill.

"But don't go there or you might meet the horrible prince who just stuffs himself with rich food all day long while we go hungry," said the boy.

"Or even worse you might meet the princess who dresses in the most expensive furs and fabrics and has five hundred pairs of shoes while poor people like us don't have even one pair between us," added the girl.

"Well, thank you for warning us," said the old man. "I really don't like the sound of that pair, do you?"

And Albert said, "Neigh."

Nevertheless, he and Albert still kept moving steadily in the direction of the big city.

Chapter 2

Pretty soon, they were over the hill and could see the city before them. The people's houses were overcrowded and falling down. The windows were broken, the doors hung off their hinges and tiles were missing from the roofs so the rain could get in. As they walked through the streets the old man and Albert saw many beggars, but nobody seemed to give them anything because the people were nearly as poor as beggars themselves. In some places they saw lines of prisoners shuffling along with chains on their necks and ankles – they were the poor people who couldn't pay the king's cruel taxes.

"I don't like this place one little bit, do you, Albert?" said the old man.

And Albert said, "Neigh."

When the old man asked directions to where the king lived, people looked frightened and warned him not to go there, but eventually he and Albert arrived at the main square and on the far side of it they saw an enormous palace.

There was a high wall round the palace with guards marching along the top, but they could still see that inside the walls there were blossoming trees and gold-covered turrets and pinnacles.

They went up to the iron gates and the old man knocked.

"I'd like to meet the royal family, please," he said.

"Meet that awful lot! Whatever for?" asked the guard, looking very surprised.

The old man pointed to the notice on the side of his cart:

ALBERT THE MAGIC HORSE
WISHES GRANTED
500 GOLD PIECES EACH
EVERY ONE A WINNER

"I want to sell them some magic wishes," he said.

"It's us poor people who need magic wishes, not this greedy royal family," exclaimed the guard. "They've got everything anybody could wish for anyway – enough food, warmth, clothes, money, a palace – everything."

"Maybe," said the old man, "but I've never met anyone yet who didn't wish for more, no matter how much they had."

"Oh, they'll wish for more all right because this is the greediest family that ever lived," said the guard.

"And don't forget my price is five hundred gold pieces," said the old man, "and from what I've seen none of the ordinary people here could afford that."

And Albert said, "Neigh."

"It still doesn't seem fair to me," said the guard, but he let them in and sent a messenger ahead to ask if the royal family would like to see this seller of magic wishes. The old man and Albert

were led through beautiful gardens full
of flowers and statues and fountains,
where strutting peacocks were the
only living creatures enjoying them.

Eventually, they were shown through the gold doors of an enormous hall, richly furnished, thickly carpeted and hung with crystal chandeliers which twinkled in the firelight. At the far end, on a platform, were four thrones.

On the biggest one sat the king. He was fat and sweating in his long robes and his heavy crown. He was counting gold pieces into a chest which was on the table at his side. The queen was even fatter and was dressed in an awful purple dress and shoes, both covered in jewels. She had a gold crown, too, and three rings on every finger. By her side sat the prince, busily scoffing a whole fruit cake from one hand, and scooping up handfuls of strawberries and ice-cream and stuffing them in his mouth with the other hand. The princess was

trying on fifty pairs of shoes, one after the other, and throwing the ones she didn't like into the fire. All in all, the royal family was not a pretty sight.

Chapter 3

"Now," snapped the king, "what's this nonsense about magic wishes? Speak up and be quick about it."

The old man pointed to the sign on his cart:

ALBERT
THE
MAGIC HORSE
WISHES GRANTED
500 GOLD PIECES
EACH
EVERY ONE A WINNER

"Every one a winner?" said the king suspiciously.

"Indeed, your majesty. You see, my magic horse Albert here" (Albert nodded his head to the king) "grants wishes. You can have as many as you like until you are satisfied, but each one costs you five hundred gold pieces."

"It's a lot of money, so this had better work!" snarled the king, as he handed over five hundred gold pieces from the chest which stood near his throne. "Now I wish for lots of gold!"

The old man nodded, went over to Albert and whispered in his ear.

And Albert said, "Neigh."

There was a sudden flash of lightning in the room and . . .

The king was frozen solid in the middle
of a gigantic ice-cube!

"Quick! Quick!" shrieked the queen, and the servants came running with hammers and axes to break up the ice and buckets and kettles of hot water to melt it. Eventually the king staggered out looking absolutely furious, but his teeth were chattering so hard he couldn't speak. He just stood dripping in front of the fire, plucking icicles out of his whiskers.

"I'm awfully sorry about that, your majesty," said the old man. "Albert's getting a bit deaf and he must have thought you said lots of COLD."

"My turn now!" said the queen, and with her plump jewelled fingers she counted out five hundred gold pieces from the chest. "I know I am very beautiful already, but even so my wish is for great glamour."

Again the old man whispered in Albert's ear.

And Albert said, "Neigh."

There was a flash of lightning and . . .

Out of the air appeared a colossal
mallet which bashed the queen over
the head and flattened her. The

Can YOU read four Young Hippo books?

YOUNG HiPPO
Readometer

★ The Young Hippo is sending a special prize to everyone who collects any four of these stickers, which can be found in Young Hippo books.

This is one sticker to stick on your own Young Hippo Readometer Card!

Collect four stickers and fill up your Readometer Card

There are all these stickers to collect too!

Get your Young Hippo Readometer Card from your local bookshop, or by sending your name and address to:

Young Hippo Readometer Card Requests, Scholastic Children's Books, 6th Floor, Commonwealth House, 1-19 New Oxford Street, London WC1A 1NU

Offer begins March 1997

servants rushed to help her to her feet and to straighten all the bent prongs on her crown. The queen was very angry indeed, but she had such a splitting headache she couldn't speak.

"Oh, tut-tut, Albert, you really must listen more carefully! I do apologize for him, your highness – he must have thought you said GREAT HAMMER."

"I'm next," said the prince, putting down a half-eaten pork pie and digging into the chest of gold pieces with his sticky hands. "And what I wish for is lots more food; for example what I fancy right now is an enormous jelly."

The old man whispered in the horse's ear.

And Albert said, "Neigh."

The flash of lightning came and . . .

The prince became fatter, and fatter, and fatter, blowing up until he was as round as a football. All his buttons went pop! and his trousers split up the seams. He rolled off his throne and bounced down the steps and across the hall. The servants caught the bouncing prince and wedged him in a corner where he very slowly deflated. He was extremely peeved, but all he could utter was a little squeak, like air coming out of a balloon.

"Now Albert, that really was too bad. I clearly said an enormous jelly, not an ENORMOUS BELLY. Now please do concentrate. I can only say I am extremely sorry, your majesties," said the old man.

"Me! Me! Me!" shrieked the princess, who had now finished with the shoes and had begun to try hats on in the mirror beside her throne. She looked in the mirror again and said, "Obviously I'm pretty, but now I wish to be very *very* pretty."

As before, the old man whispered to
Albert.

And Albert said, "Neigh."

The lightning flashed and . . .

. . . nothing seemed to change – most certainly the princess did not become prettier. Instead she began to scratch.

She threw away her crown and had a good tear at her hair. Then she tore off her jewels and shoes and dress and underclothes and scratched and scritched away at every limb. She jumped up and down and howled as the servants sprayed her with flea powder and dunked her head in a bucket of water. She really was hopping mad, but the flea powder had got up her nose and all she could do was sneeze and sneeze.

"Oh, deary, deary me, Albert, how ever could you mistake pretty for NITTY? He really can do better than this, your majesties, I promise you. Now, would anybody like to try again?"

Angry as they all were, the royal family could see that Albert really did have magic powers, so they all had another turn. And, of course, they paid five hundred gold pieces for each wish.

This time the king wished for great power and was instantly soaked by a GREAT SHOWER which poured cold water on him. He had only just got warm after his ice-cube experience and now his teeth were chattering again.

The queen tried once more and this time she wished for a lot of money. She immediately found herself covered in HONEY and it took a long time to chase all the angry bees away. The servants had to scrape the sticky mess off her with spoons.

The royal family were extremely cross by this time.

Chapter 4

"Your magic horse has messed up every wish we've made," shouted the king. "Now you've one last chance before I send you both off to prison!"

"I really can't understand it, your majesties. Things don't usually go wrong when people make their magic wishes, do they, Albert?" said the old man.

And Albert said, "Neigh."

Now the prince and princess were both greedy, but they weren't stupid. They had a think and a whisper together and then the prince said to the old man: "I can see there's some real magic at work here, but it keeps going wrong every time we wish for something for ourselves. This time I want to try my wish out on somebody else first and see what happens to them."

"What a good idea, your majesty," said the old man, as he took yet another five hundred gold pieces from the prince.

"Follow me," said the prince, and he led the king, queen, princess, the old man and Albert out on to the balcony which overlooked the city. From there they could see the main square where the poor people were going about their miserable lives.

"See that poor thin man shopping in the market there? The one followed by all his hungry children?" asked the prince. "Right, my wish is that they could enjoy a feast fit for a prince."

The old man smiled and whispered in Albert's ear, and Albert said, "Yea."

There was a flash of lightning and . . .

The poor man was suddenly loaded with shopping bags full of fruits and vegetables and meats and cheeses and jams and cakes. All his children found their arms full of wonderful things to eat and drink. They were astonished and set off laughing for home to cook a feast for all their family and friends.

"Now, that time my wish did come true," said the prince, "and didn't those poor people look happy!"

"Now it's my turn again," said the princess. "You see that beggar woman dressed in rags by the palace gates? My wish is that she is clothed as finely and warmly as a princess."

Well, the old man smiled and whispered in Albert's ear.

And Albert said, "Yea."

There was a flash of lightning and . . .

The beggar woman was instantly
dressed in warm, bright, clean clothes
with fine boots and even a hat with a
curly feather in it. She looked down

at herself in amazement, then went dancing joyfully across the square to show everyone how her fortune had miraculously changed.

"That was fun," said the princess. "I'd never realized how nice it is to help people like that."

Chapter 5

The king and queen began to get the idea now. The queen said, "You see that tumble-down dressmaker's house across the square? The one with holes in the roof and broken windows? I wish that it could be made into a beautiful dwelling fit for a queen."

And it was. The roof sprouted lovely red tiles, the windows had glass and

curtains, the paintwork shone and a beautiful garden sprang up all around it. The dressmaker came out of her new front door looking astonished, and then invited people inside to look at her wonderful new house.

"I enjoyed that," said the queen, "and wouldn't it be marvellous if everybody had a house like that!"

Next, the king said, "I wish those wretched prisoners tramping past the palace gates could lose their chains and be free."

And they were. They looked at their bare wrists and ankles in surprise, then

laughed and danced all round the square with glee. A lot more people joined in, and soon there was a large crowd cheering and dancing in the square below the balcony.

"Well," said the king, "that wish made a lot of people feel better, including me."

Then the four royal personages went to one side and had a little discussion.

"Have you noticed," asked the princess, "that if you wish for something just for yourself the wish goes wrong?"

"And if you wish for something good for somebody else," observed the prince, "then the wish is granted."

"And wasn't it nice to see all those folk being happy instead of miserable for a change?" said the queen.

"Yes, it was," agreed the king. "Let's ask the old man if we can wish for more good things for the poor."

Then they returned to the old man and Albert.

"Could I wish that ALL our people had warm, clean clothes to wear?" asked the princess.

"Could I wish that ALL the people had enough to eat?" asked the prince.

"Could I wish that ALL the people could earn enough money to live on?" asked the queen.

And the king asked the old man, "Could I wish that everybody in our country could learn to like us?"

"Well, yes," said the old man. "Of course you can wish for all these things, if you really want them."

"We do, we do, we do, we do," they said.

"But unfortunately Albert cannot grant them," said the old man.

"Oh no! Why not?" asked the king in dismay.

"Look," said the old man. "Your chest has no gold pieces left in it to buy any more wishes."

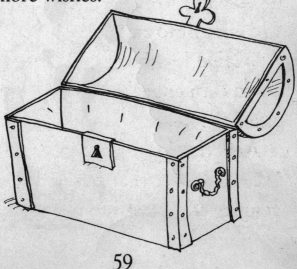

And Albert said, "Neigh."

"I'll sell all my jewels to buy some more wishes," said the queen.

"I'll go on a diet and use the money I save to buy more wishes," said the prince.

"And I'll sell all my silly fancy clothes," said the princess.

"Yes, you should certainly do all these things, but I'm afraid poor Albert has no more magic left in him at the moment."

And Albert shook his head and said, "Neigh."

"Then what are we to do to help all our people?" asked the king in despair.

"Well, if you think about it, your majesty," said the old man, "you can grant every one of those wishes yourself without using any magic at all."

And he and Albert left the room, and the palace.

When it was dark, the old man went round the town putting gold pieces through the letter-boxes until they were all shared out. Then he and Albert

travelled on to the next place where people needed to learn how to use their wishes properly.

As they left the country, the old man said, "I don't think the people here will be cold and ragged and hungry any more, do you, Albert?"

And Albert said, "Neigh."